The Asylum for ~~~~ ๅge
and T~
(Tales of ๅ ~~~~ *nseen)*

The Tales included within are:

1

The Asylum for the Strange and the Different

Part 1. Mother and Son.

Once upon a time... many, many years ago in a world long since forgotten, there was a country called Anywhere. And in the land of Anywhere there was a fine and prosperous city called Anyplace and in this fine city lived a woman who had three children, two girls and a boy.

Unfortunately for the children The Woman was a person of inordinate selfishness, one of those people who feel that they world revolves around them and them alone, someone who was prepared to do anything to get what she wanted. To make things worse, the children had lost their father at an early age. The poor man had died of a broken heart for during the course of his marriage to The Woman he had come to realise that she had not married him for love but simply as a way of escaping from her own background (which had been rather Poor And Mean) and gaining Financial Security and Social Standing. For his own reasons, which to this day remain unfathomable, the husband had loved The Woman dearly and simply could not reconcile the love he felt for her with the total lack of love she had for him. So he succumbed to the Sadness Disease (which in your world you call cancer) but beat it to its fatal conclusion by drinking himself to death.

This left three children (another unfathomable question that also remains unanswered to this day – exactly why did she have children?) to be raised by one very strange woman. The Woman only had two Real Loves and they were Social Standing and

Gambling. She loved nothing more than praise and attention from friends, associates and The Neighbours and, in pursuit of such, would portray herself to those around her as a brave and valiant Single Mother who Devoted Her Life to raising and caring for her darling children, and such performance did indeed bring her much praise and her precious, desired Social Standing.

But The Woman's Truth as she presented it to the world was a Fiction. The Woman's children were left pretty much to bring up themselves, she was an Absent And Unconcerned parent for her love for herself and her needs was too great to spare any love for her children. She put (some) food on the table and (some) clothes on the children's backs but nothing else. And then not always, for almost every cent and penny that came into the household was spent on The Woman's other Great Love: gambling. Oh, how The Woman loved to gamble, for hours and days on end. She would gamble on horses, dogs, rabbits, flashing lights – anything that moved and presented a chance of a chance!

Growing up with this strange, self-obsessed woman was difficult for all three children but most particularly for The Boy. Girls are always cleverer about these things and The Boy's sisters had long since recognised The Mother for the Selfish And Uncaring creature she was and they had simply resolved to get on with life until such time as they were old enough to leave home and never come back. The Boy felt things more keenly for, like his father, he had, for yet another unfathomable reason to this day unexplained, a Deep And Abiding Love for his mother. And he desperately wanted her to return that love, to share a kind word, a warm embrace. Of course, The Woman never did any of these things but the more she showed The Boy that she had no love for him, the more he wanted her to love him and the harder he would try to be loved and he would say:

'Look at this, Mum',

'I love you, Mum',

'Look what we did at school today, Mum.'

'You look nice today, Mum.'

'I made this for you, Mum.'

And The Woman would grunt and turn her back on him and return to her gambling or telling stories to The Neighbours of her sacrifices for her children as a struggling Single Mother.

Truth be told, The Woman didn't just not love her son, she despised him. She saw him as a threat to her Social Standing for whilst The Boy had a pleasing and loving nature and was not unintelligent or untalented (indeed he had a beautiful singing voice) or unattractive, he was small for his fourteen years and had a certain gentle feyness about him – a degree of femininity that she disliked and distrusted. She was very concerned that the child might be a *falulah* (a 'falulah' is Anywhere slang that corresponds to words like 'queer' and 'faggot' in your world).

Now, this Tale is set in some years back in the history of Anywhere, before the brief Golden Age and social, cultural and economic blooming that occurred as a result of breaking the dead grip of The Greedy One Percent (sadly short-lived though that period was) and Social Attitudes were, particularly on matters of difference and sexuality, still very retarded – being identified as a falulah was a matter of great Social Embarrassment and shame and it was widely considered that a person was better off dead than falulah.

So - The Mother's suspicions that her son might be 'one of them' caused her considerable concern. Imagine the Social

Shame of having a son who was inclined that way. What would the neighbours think? And the damage such shame would cause to her Social Standing! Unacceptable!

Then one day all The Woman's fears were confirmed for The Boy came back from school with a ripped shirt and a bloody lip and tears in his eyes. 'Mum,' he said, 'the other boys beat me and laughed at me and called me a falulah, why mum, why?'

And a spasm of pure terror and shame shot through The Woman. See, she had been right, the boy was a fulalah and now other people were beginning to notice! Oh, the shame, all those years of building up her Social Standing were going to be ruined by this horrible, useless falulah child.

'Well, I'm not surprised,' said the infuriated mother, 'I mean look at you, you're pathetic, you're so small, you're tiny compared to the other boys and you sound like a girl. Huh, they're right you are a falulah!' With these words she walked towards her child and The Boy, despite her harsh words, thought (or at least fervently hoped) that she was going to comfort him. Instead she stopped short of The Boy, raised a hand above her head and slammed it down with all her strength across his face, knocking him to the floor. 'Get upstairs to your room!' she screamed. And as the terrified child did just that, she screamed after him:

'Dwarf!'

'Midget!'

'Falulah!'

'Falulah!'

Calming herself, The Mother thought about what she should do. A falulah for a son, what a humiliation. She couldn't let this miserable child threaten her Social Standing – but short of murdering the child (which, to be quite frank, she would have done were it not for the fear of being caught) what could be done? And she thought. And she thought. And she thought. And she came up with a plan.

The next day, whilst The Boy was at school, she made her way to The Asylum For The Strange And The Different.

Part 2. The Asylum For The Strange And The Different.

To understand what happened next in this tale it is necessary to understand about The Asylum For The Strange And The Different and its position in Anywhere's society at this point in Anywhere's history. Fundamentally, it was a dumping ground – for The Strange and The Different – The Strange being those considered to be mad and The Different being those who didn't quite fit in with society because they perhaps had strange views and ideas, or whose politics were regarded as dangerous or who were, perhaps, falulahs.

Once an unfortunate individual was placed in The Asylum, that was it, They were gone. Lost. Invisible. Never to be heard from again. No inmates of The Asylum ever left that grim place alive.

And The Asylum was truly dreadful, a black pit of madness and despair: those who worked there only worked there as a very last resort, out of desperation to earn some kind of living. Faeries would not fly within a two mile radius of it and Trolls would not even mention it in conversation (to do so was considered to bring the worst of luck): even Death was a reluctant to go there, though The Devil did think it rather a fun place to visit. Certainly nobody ever came to see anybody at The Asylum; after all it was where Strange or Difficult people were dumped and why, having got rid of them, would one want to visit them?

Within the walls of The Asylum there was no concept of treatment or care for its reluctant inmates. The Different were there simply to keep their disturbing ideas and proclivities away from wider society – that was all, nothing to do but keep them locked away until they died. The Different – they were just mad and there was nothing to done about that: in the land of Anywhere at this time madness was considered not be an illness or dysfunction but an Altered State. The belief was that mad people were mad because they had, in some way, communed with The Devil. During the course of their congress with Satan, he had allowed them to open the pages of his Book Of The Dead. The Devil's Book Of The Dead is a kind of Satanic Stamp Album. An album of huge size and length in which The Devil, the Ultimate Connoisseur Of Suffering, records (for his delight and delectation) the saddest of deaths – those being to The Devil (and to your narrator) the premature deaths, be it by disease or violence, of The Young And The Innocent. And each death is recorded not in words, instead it is written in emotion, in the pain and sadness that was endured in the course of that death. As such, The Devil's Book Of Death contains a depth of pain so great, so deep, so profound that to open even one page for one second is enough to plunge any man or woman into madness, a madness that is pure and unchangeable – an Altered State. All that is to be done with a person who has peered into The Devil's Book Of Death is to assign them until death to The Asylum For The Strange And The Different.

So, there you have it, The Asylum For The Strange And The Different was no more or no less than a place where those considered mad, different, awkward or embarrassing were sent to die. Once in, there was no way out except death. To be an inmate in The Asylum was to 'live' in a state of non-existence.

Let's return now to my little tale. Having been informed of the nature and purpose of The Asylum For The Strange And The Different you've probably guessed the purpose of The Mother's visit there. That's right, she'd gone there to visit the Director of The Asylum to plead her case for having The Boy admitted (dumped and forgotten until death) there. All in all, things went well for her. The Director, a miserable bigot of a man who abhorred difference of any kind and particularly falulahs, had agreed with her. Her case was justified, keeping a falulah in the family home would indeed result in Unacceptable Embarrassment to her with a concomitant drop in her Social Status. However, just to oil the wheels, smooth the path and get The Boy admitted the next day might she consider a Small Token Of Her Appreciation, maybe just lie back and lift up her skirt, just twenty minutes of her time?

The Mother considered the Director's request to have sex with her and thought, why not if it's going to get the job done and get that horrible child out my life? The decision was made all the easier to make because on the way to The Asylum she had suddenly realised another 'plus' of getting rid of The Boy: one less mouth to feed would mean more money for one of the true loves of her life – gambling! Don't be shocked, I did tell you she was a truly awful woman...

The next day, The Boy was getting ready for school (The Boy and his sister's always got themselves ready for school, The Mother never being awake that early in the day due to having been up late gambling) when, much to his surprise his mother appeared, fully dressed, bright and smiling.

'Well hullo, my little man!' she said cheerily, 'and how are
you today? My son, my beloved son, you've been having a
difficult time so today there'll be no school – you're coming to
the shops with me and we're going to buy you a treat and then
we'll go for a lovely Sludge burger!'

And The Boy beamed from ear to ear, for this was Heaven to
him, at last his mother was being nice to him, the only thing he
really, really wanted in life was finally coming to pass!

The Boy and his mother jumped into a clarb (the Anywhere
equivalent of a London black cab) and began their journey. The
Mother explained to The Boy that before they went to the shops
she just had to stop off somewhere and 'pick something up for
a friend.' The Boy nodded and smiled and took hold of his
mother's hand and squeezed it gently. This vaguely repulsed The
Mother but she accepted it, even squeezed The Boy's hand gently
back – keep the horrible little thing happy and quiet, she
thought, I'll soon be rid of it, she thought.

By and by, the clarb came to, you've guessed it, The Asylum
For The Strange And The Difficult, and the mother said 'come
on, little man, come with me – this thing I have to collect is quite
heavy so you can give me a hand!'

Willingly The Boy jumped out of the clarb with his mother,
happy to help. Seeing the huge, grey, bleak, hulking building
before him he felt a sense of doom and despair but comforted
himself with the thought that he was with his mother, she'd
make sure that everything was fine.

Into The Asylum went mother and soon. Down long,
depressing corridors painted that sickly, pale shade of green
beloved by bureaucracies in all worlds everywhere, until they
came to a blank, anonymous looking door. 'Ah, yes,' said the

mother, 'this is where we should be – be a dear and pop into this room will you and pick up the package there...' and she swung open that anonymous door. And The Boy, eager to please, entered the room and before he could register the fact that it contained no package, two burly Asylum employees threw a thick, heavy net over him and wrestled him to the ground, dragging him out of the room and down, down, down another long, depressing corridor and as he kicked and screamed and was hauled away to a state of non-existence oh, how the mother laughed and she shouted:

'Idiot!'

'Midget!'

'Girl!'

'Falulah!'

'Falulah!'

And The Boy cried:

'Mummy!'

'No, mummy, no!'

'Why, mummy?'

'Why?'

'Why....'

And The Boy carried on crying out for his mother all the way down into the rotten bowels of The Asylum and carried on crying out when thrown into a dank, dark cell by which time his only audience was four blank walls.

Later that day, back at home, a jubilant mother would put on a sad face (for she was adept at putting on different faces at different times for different people) and tell her daughters that their brother had run away to sea in search of adventure and had told her he would never be back. The sisters had long since learned that not a single word that came out of the mouth of their mother could be trusted but they questioned not, for they were also aware that their mother was a Dangerous Woman. They simply accepted that, whatever had happened to their brother, he would Never Be Seen Again: they would spend a lifetime quietly mourning his loss.

The Boy would spend 25 years in The Asylum For The Strange And The Different. He survived so long because that first night in his lonely cell he faced A Truth Too Difficult To Bear. Hopefully, reader, you've not come across A Truth Too Difficult To Bear in your own life, so let me explain...

At times, if we're unlucky, The Blind Old Weaver Of Fate randomly weaves into the story of our lives some threads that are so bitter and so painful that we simply cannot face them, cannot accept them. So we ignore them. However, we cannot ignore the pain that those random, unpleasant threads cause us and that pain does not go away. Being fundamentally rational beings we then have to invent another reason for that pain we are feeling and the circumstances we're in, some reason other than The Truth That Is Too Difficult To Bear.

The Boy went through this process. Alone, there in a cell. Abandoned by a mother he was desperate to be loved by, abandoned for being a falulah. What fourteen year old boy would not find that A Truth Too Difficult To Bear? So The Boy found a different reason to explain away his Truth That Was Too Difficult To Bear. He forgot, completely and deliberately, that his mother had called him a falulah. But he remembered he had said she was small. And that was it, that was why she was not with him and why he was in this horrible place, he had simply ended up here by mistake as his mother had lost him because he was so small and she could not find him because he was so small that she couldn't see him! But she was looking for him every day and would carry on looking for him until she found him because she missed him so much!

And that chain of logic gave him hope and a reason to carry on living. For, surely, if he ate lots and lots and lots he would grow bigger and bigger and eventually he would be so big that his mother would be able to see him and find him and they would be reunited!

The Boy spent the next twenty five years in The Asylum eating and eating. He discovered that if he shouted and screamed then The Asylum guards would (wanting a quiet life) give him food to shut him up. He also discovered that if he sang guards and inmates would give him more food to carry on singing for he had always had a good singing voice but now his internal pain had lent it a supernatural beauty.

So, for twenty five years he sang, shouted, screamed and, mostly, ate and ate and ate. By the eve of his fortieth birthday he was, as you say in your world, as big as a house – grossly, morbidly and fatally obese. And on that day, the eve of his birthday, he awoke in the morning, took a few steps and fell to the ground, a pain in his chest, gasping for breath. Straight away he knew what was happening, he knew his long broken heart was failing but he was not afraid, he was ecstatic for he knew that his heart was failing because he was so fat. He was so....huge! And being so huge, well his mother could not fail to see him now, could she? She would see him and come to him and make his heart better and wipe away all the years of pain and abandonment and all would be well and he would be with his mummy again and she would love him so very, very much!

With his last breathes The Boy called out:

'Mummy, look at me, look how big I am!'

'You can see me know, can't you mummy?

'Mummy?'

'Can you see me?'

'Can you see me?'

'Mummy?'

'Mummy...'

'Mummy...'

'Are you there...'

'MUMMY!'

'PLEASE! PLEASE SEE ME!'

And there was silence.

And then...

The Boy stopped feeling sad and lonely and scared and Abandoned for he realised that he had done nothing wrong, that he was not wrong, that he was a beautiful creation of God and God and life and love and the Universe loved him; there was no Sin on his side – that was all on his mother's side for she was an uncaring, unfeeling selfish monster. And with that thought he was free and he understood that the best chapters of his journey were still to be written...he was on his way to some where better and up ahead of him he sees fascinating, flashing coloured lights and he knows, just knows, that they are disco lights and he can hear a song with a thumping beat that makes him want to dance and he knows, just knows, that it's disco music and that the song is called 'You Make Me Feel (Mighty Real)', that the artist is called Sylvester and, boy, does he love it!

And so...

The Boy emerges, kicking and screaming with delight and anticipation, into the welcoming light of a brand new day.

'A Lunatic and a Fool!'

'Strange times are these in which we live when old and young are taught falsehoods...and the person that dares to tell the truth is called at once a lunatic and a fool' -**Plato**

Once upon a time in the land of Anywhere, in a world long since forgotten, in the fine and prosperous city of Anyplace there was a shop. A shoe shop to be precise. The shop was successful and highly regarded, run by a much respected old Shoemaker who lived above the premises and who made all the shoes himself, working from a cramped little studio at the back of the building.

The Shoemaker's creations were very popular with the residents of Anyplace. His men's shoes were considered hard wearing and durable, yet stylish. His shoes for ladies were seen as the height of wit and whimsy and the very pinnacle of fashion. Over the years he had built up a considerable clientele and become very comfortably off.

Now, one bright, sunny day, The Shoemaker was taking a break from shoe selling and shoe making and was enjoying a stroll through the pleasant surrounds of Anyplace's finest public space, The Park Of A Thousand Joyous Souls. As he walked he contemplated the fine views afforded by the park, admired the beautiful statue of the famous Ragged Man (who's song had shaken a Kingdom) and felt, generally, delighted to be alive. But his Happy Reverie was to be rudely interrupted. Walking past an area of the park thick with bushes and long grass, he thought he heard someone crying. Listen. There it is again. Over there!

Being a Kind And Considerate Soul, The Shoemaker decided that he must investigate the Source Of This Sadness. Pushing himself into the long grass and thick bushes he battled his way towards who, or what, was making such a plaintive noise. And...much to his surprise came across a Faerie. Sitting in a tree. Crying. Tears rolling down her pretty face, each one turning into a tiny diamond as it did so (as Faerie tears do), and then dropping to the ground; a sharp, hard piece of glittering sorrow.

"Why, Faerie, what's all this then, why the tears?" said The Shoemaker, peering upwards at the tree branch upon which the Faerie was sitting.

"A dog...a dog...a dog ate my shoes! I took them of just for a moment to bathe my feet in a stream, looked back and there was a dog...with my shoes in his mouth...then he swallowed them and ran off! Oh...I loved those shoes!"

"Oh, poor you, that is a sad story. But, Faerie, it's your lucky day, for I am a shoemaker, one of some renown even though I say so myself. Come with me and I shall make you a beautiful new pair of shoes that you shall come to love even more than those you've just lost!"

"Really?" enquired the Faerie, hopefully.

"Really!" responded The Shoemaker, affirmatively.

And off they went, man and Faerie. Before they left on their Quest the Faerie asked The Shoemaker (aware of their value in the Human World) if he'd like to collect her diamond tears that were lying, sparkling, in the grass. The Shoemaker replied, thank you, but no...he was already very blessed in life and one of his blessings was Financial Security...better, then, to leave the Faerie diamonds to be found by someone who needed them more. Such was The Calibre Of The Man.

By and by, the Faerie and the man found themselves back in The Shoemaker's shop.

"Sit yourself down there, Faerie, let's have a look at those feet of yours."

"Oohh..." said The Shoemaker.

"Ahhh..." said The Shoemaker, for the Faeries feet were Very, Very Small, "excuse me just one minute, Faerie."

The Shoemaker stood up and popped next door to see his friend, The Watchmaker.

Quickly he returned, bringing with him a fine and delicate set of watchmaker's tools, the only tools he could think of that would be small enough to fashion a pair of shoes for a pair of tiny Faerie feet.

"So, Faerie, I now have The Tools I Need To Do The Job! Tell me, what do you like to see in a pair of shoes?"

The Faerie looked back at The Shoemaker, thoughtfully pondering the Desired Utility And Properties Of Shoes and said:

"Comfort."

"Durability."

"Colour!"

"Stylishness!"

"Stiletto heels!"

"Ahh, Faerie, you are indeed a person...well, mmm, a Faeire...after my own heart! Come, let's look at my leather stocks and see what tickles your fancy."

In terms of leather, The Shoemaker recommended to the Faerie a fine Epicurean Leather from the land of Otherplace. Generally held to be the Finest Leather known, Epicurean Leather is soft yet strong and has a dazzling, glossy red finish.

When The Shoemaker showed a sample of it to the Faerie, her eyes and mouth opened wide and she let out an awed "ohhh, yes!" and fluttered her wings in excitement.

Thus the leather for the Faeire's new shoes was chosen and The Shoemaker began his work and, using the fine set of watchmaker's tools and a magnifying glass, he had, by the end of the day, fashioned a pair of truly beautiful, stylish red shoes with stiletto heels that were both stylish and comfortable. 'To die for', I believe you would say in your own world...

All in all, The Shoemaker thought this pair of tiny shoes was probably the most beautiful he had ever fashioned. And the Faerie agreed, she was absolutely delighted - cock-a-hoop with pleasure, even.

And here's where our tale really begins. For the Faerie was very grateful to The Shoemaker, not just for the beautiful new shoes he had made her but for his Kindness And Solicitude in general and, being bound by the Faerie code of 'a good deed done is a good deed earned' she passed to him a very interesting piece of advice.

She told him: "Shoemaker, you must stop making pairs of shoes. From this day forth you must only make left foot shoes, and those only in a size seven, for the time is coming when these are the only shoes that people will want."

The Shoemaker raised his eyebrows at this extraordinary and strange statement and replied, "why do you tell me this, Faerie? It is a very, very strange thing to say...forgive me, but I have to ask you directly – is the statement you've just made the absolute truth?"

And that was very wise thing for The Shoemaker to ask for, if you are a student of the land of Anywhere, you'll already know that Faeries have a Duality Of Nature. They can be very, very good or they can be downright mischievous. And if they should cast for you a Faerie spell, well, you'd better watch yourself for even when Faeries try their very best to cast a spell that is wholly good a Degree Of Duality (which can represent a substantial sting in the tale of said spell) will always tend to creep into the mix. So, always be cautious when a Faerie makes Magick or tells you something that seems of interest to you. Fortunately, The Shoemaker was wise enough to know all this. He was also wise enough to know that Faeries are bound by the same Universal Principle as The Devil - in that if you ask either a Direct Question they have no choice but to answer honestly.

Thus when the Faerie confirmed the veracity of her statement, The Shoemaker knew that the comment about size seven, left foot shoes was absolutely and undeniably true but, as he said farewell to a very happy Faerie, he pondered where on Earth he should go with the information? Should he follow the Faerie's advice and do something that really was quite odd and would, no doubt, impact upon his life in a major way? Or should he simply ignore what the Faerie had told him – in the knowledge that it's rarely a good idea to ignore what a Faerie tells you if you know it to be truth?

The Shoemaker pondered hard and long. And came to a decision. Faeries were basically good creatures. The Faerie said make only size seven, left foot shoes for a reason and The Shoemaker felt convinced that that reason would eventually be revealed to him and, despite any struggles encountered along on the way, it would be for the good. From that point, he decided, he would devote his efforts to making only size seven, left foot shoes.

Which is exactly what The Shoemaker did. After holding a huge Clearance Sale to get rid of stock to make way for his new line of size seven, left foot shoes he began to make said shoes. He made shoe after shoe, day after day, exhausting his stocks of leather so he had to buy in more. He made size seven, left foot shoes for ladies, for men, with high heels and flat heels in black and brown and red and blue. He even briefly experimented with platform heels, but quickly decided they were an abomination and abandoned that particular experiment.

Days turned into weeks and weeks turned into months. And still The Shoemaker carried on doggedly following the Faerie's advice. His shop was now full to the rafters with size seven, left foot shoes of every conceivable style, type or fashion and size seven, left foot shoes also filled the rooms The Shoemaker lived in above the shop, his workshop and the shop's back yard. And The Shoemaker's business and reputation had been destroyed. No-one visited his shop anymore (why would anyone want to buy just one shoe for one foot in one size?) and people would see him in the street and Point At Him And Laugh. He had gone from being a respected shoemaker to being 'that mad old cobbler' (and, trust me on this, nothing wounds a shoemaker so much as being called a cobbler). Even his 'friends' had abandoned him (for being Socially Embarrassing). Where once they had talked of him warmly, they now described him as a 'lunatic and a fool'.

With No Money Coming In, The Shoemaker was forced to buy new leather and pay all his Living Costs from his savings and where once he had been prosperous he became poor. Yet still he had faith in his decision and the Faerie's advice.

Meanwhile, The Blind Old Weaver Of Fate, as the Faerie knew she would, had spun together some threads that would justify the Faerie's advice and The Shoemaker's Faith And Persistence.

For in a heavily guarded, secret Military Industrial Complex situated on the outskirts of Anyplace, a team of Evil Scientists in the employ of The Greedy One Percent had developed a Genetically Modified Virus. This virus was designed to be harmless to humans, but fatal to Trolls (hence it's codename: TROLLKILL). The Greedy One Percent's hope was that, once released into the environment, the virus would soon wipe out Anywhere's entire Troll population - freeing up their lands (which the Banker class has always coveted) for Redevelopment Purposes.

However very little, if anything, occurs in the land of Anywhere that is not Observed, Noted, Annotated and Judged by Faeries. And the evil that was unfolding in the secret Military Industrial Complex was no exception. Borne upon The Wings Of A Faerie, news of The Greedy One Percent's evil plan (and the location of the secret Military Industrial Complex) soon reached the Troll Community. The Trolls were not disturbed by the thought of the TROLLKILL virus - for Trolls are wise and far seeing creatures who were well aware that the virus would not work properly. After all, it had been produced by the Military Industrial Complex which was deeply incompetent and more about enriching itself with tax-payer's money than producing anything that was actually effective. That said, it was still decided by a specially convened Troll Grand Council, that Something Should Be Done to let humans know that this kind of Nefarious Behaviour was not acceptable and would Not Go Unpunished.

The very next day, the secret Military Industrial Complex was subject to a Mass Troll Depredation. Guards and scientists and Civilian Contractors alike were offered the choice of being ripped apart by angry Trolls or Fleeing The Scene (they sensibly all chose to flee as you, too, would have done. There are few thing more scary in life than an angry Troll! The entire complex was then set to flame.

Now, by burning the Complex the Trolls had hoped to destroy the TROLLKILL virus and prevent any further work on it. But their plan was not entirely successful: a small amount of TROLLKILL made it into the atmosphere. Picked up by a strong wind, the virus was blown over the city of Anyplace. With catastrophic results. But for humans, not Trolls. Humans, you see, are not half as clever as they think they are, and once they stray into the area of Genetic Modification, messing around with the building blocks of life (a secret code known only to God and The Devil and as old as Time Itself) Unintended Consequences are bound to arise.

In this case, the Unintended Consequence became very apparent very quickly as, within the period of just a day, the entire human population of the city of Anyplace came down with a sore throat, a mild fever and an excruciating pain in both feet. The sore throat and mild fever soon passed, but the pain in both feet continued until the left foot had shrunk (or grown) to a size seven whilst the right foot simply rotted and dropped off leaving behind a perfectly healed stump.

When The Shoemaker noticed that he had a sore throat and slight fever, he thought he was coming down with flu (though the pain in the feet thing was a bit odd!), as if he didn't have enough to worry about with no money and barely enough to eat! But, when he noticed his left foot shrinking to a size seven and his right foot dropping off to leave a perfectly healed stump, he was elated. Perhaps this was it! Finally, the Faeries words had been proven truthful and his dedication and persistence fruitful!

And it was indeed 'it'! In no time at all, The Shoemaker's shop was besieged by an entire city's populace, desperate for size seven, left foot shoes! The Shoemaker did a roaring trade and, following the Principles Of Capitalism and the Law Of Supply And Demand (and to gain a rather satisfying revenge against people who had mocked and belittled him), he increased the price of his shoes massively, making an Extremely Healthy Margin on each shoe he sold.

So it was that The Shoemaker once again became a rich and respected man, and the day he suddenly started to make only size eight, right foot shoes, nobody mocked him, not at all.

Nora-Lee's Story

Once upon a time... many, many years ago in a world long since forgotten, there was a country called Anywhere. And in the land of Anywhere there was a fine and prosperous city called Anyplace and in this fine city lived two sisters, Dora-Lee and Nora-Lee.

Now Dora-Lee was the oldest sister by a year and she was a beautiful girl, the apple of her parents eye for she was graceful and beautiful; a great favourite with the boys. Nora-Lee was the younger sister. But...poor Nora-Lee, she was, at best, a plain girl, a bit chubby and somewhat clumsy. Her parents found Nora-Lee an embarrassment, she was certainly not a favourite with the boys; she wasn't even allowed to see them, the family preferring to keep Nora-Lee hidden away as much as possible. The fact that Nora-Lee was actually by far the nicer and kinder of the two sisters, the fact that the plain wrapper of her body concealed a sharp and remarkable intelligence. Well, all that counted for naught in the eyes of her parents and wider society; judgements about what makes a woman being as facile and stupid in the land of Anywhere as in your own world.

Nora-Lee had recently celebrated (celebrated not really being an apt word as the day had actually passed by unremarked by all) her eighteenth birthday. She was now a young woman and wanted to assert her own position and personality in the world.

But she simply could not do it. For she was only Nora-Lee, the plain, chubby and clumsy sister of the beautiful Dora-Lee. Her life, such as it was, was lived in the shadow of her sister, whatever she did or said, she was always compared to Dora-Lee and was always found wanting.

If Nora-Lee wore a beautiful dress, people would say:

"Oh, Nora-Lee, look at you, what a mess! Don't you know a fat woman should not wear a tight dress! Oh, Nora-Lee, Nora-Lee why can't you be more like Dora-Lee!"

If Nora-Lee tried to engage in conversation, people would say:

"Oh, Nora-Lee, shut up, what a bore! Don't you know how dull you are, don't talk any more! Oh, Nora-Lee, Nora-Lee why can't you be more like Dora-Lee!"

If Nora-Lee suggested that she too would like to see boys, people would say:

"Oh, Nora-Lee, you must be mad! Don't you know a boy would never want to see a girl who looks so bad! Oh, Nora-Lee, Nora-Lee why can't you be more like Dora-Lee!"

If Nora-Lee cooked a nice meal people would say:

"Oh, Nora-Lee, you are so thick. This food you've made is disgusting and it tastes like sick! Oh, Nora-Lee, Nora-Lee why can't you be more like Dora-Lee."

If Nora-Lee expressed ambition people would say:

"Oh, Nora-Lee, don't be so keen! You are a plain and clumsy girl, life for you will be hard and the pickings will be lean! Oh, Nora-Lee, Nora-Lee why can't you be more like Dora-Lee!"

If Nora-Lee asked her sister if they could do something together, Dora-Lee would say:

"Oh, Nora-Lee, are you insane! I am so pretty and you are so plain, to spend time with you would be an embarrassment and a pain. Oh, Nora-Lee, Nora-Lee, why can't you be more like me!"

One cold winter's day it occurred to Nora-Lee that she was desperately sad and more than a bit mad. She knew that she would never get to be the person she really wanted be, her life would always be found wanting compared to that of the Fabulous Dora-Lee.

Like a flower growing in the shade she would never make the grade, she would grow up weak and sickly and live a stunted life of unfulfilled possibility, sacrificed on the altar of the stunning Dora-Lee.

Staring out of the window of her small and tatty attic room, where she passed most of her time, Nora-Lee began to think what she might do. How would she ever be free of Dora-Lee?

And then it began to snow.

Peering outside at an all too familiar view, Nora-Lee saw the snow coming down thick and fast. In a matter of only minutes, Nora-Lee's vista changed from same old streets and houses to a glistening, fresh, new Wonderland Of White. A New World of New Possibility. Nora-Lee allowed herself a rare smile. For if something as Fixed And Immutable as the very landscape itself could be Changed So Quickly into something so new and different, could not a life, too, be so changed?

The very next day when the beautiful Dora-Lee was trying on one of her gorgeous dresses Nora-Lee snuck up behind her sister and emptied last night's chamber pot, full of wee and pooh over her head.

With her sister staring at her in disbelief and horror, wee pouring down her face, bits of pooh stuck in her hair, Nora-Lee thought to herself:

"Oh dear, my sister stands before me, smeared in wee and pooh by my own hand. I should be sorry and sad, but I don't feel bad. Rather, I feel really very grand for finally I have rebelled and now I know I can be the person I was always meant to be. In a word, I am free."

Finishing that thought, Nora-Lee left the family home and went out into the world to make her own life, married a beautiful Prince (or maybe a Princess?) and lived happily ever after.

And the moral of this tale is: never let the life you live be decided by other peoples' perception of you. Live the life you want to live and be the person you were always meant to be.

For Nora-Lee

Here's to boys who like boys, girls who like girls and men who like to wear dresses. Here's to the woman who doesn't want to look like an anorexic stick insect from some vile fashion magazine and who knows she is the equal of any man. Here's to the man who is man enough to know what 'being a man' really means, the man who is comfortable in his own skin and who doesn't give shit to anyone or take shit from no-one. Here's to those who don't have any interest in telling others how to live their lives but have an interest in the lives of others, those who can shed a tear for their fellows, who know it's not always about "me, me, me" and always remember that "there but for the grace of God go I." Here's to those who recognise the Power of Love and know that the life we live in this world is but a small fraction of our total existence.

Here's to those who will not accept that a system that hands out opportunity and privilege based on how rich your parents are is neither justified nor justifiable, to those who believe in a level playing field for all. Here's to those who are, every day and in every way, angry with the world even in the face of their own powerlessness and who don't know when to shut up about it, refusing to go quietly into the night. Here's to those who aren't ready to be the people other people think they should be, who just won't dress appropriately for their age or do the "sensible" thing. Here's to those who don't believe a word they are told, who will always check the "facts" and the "research" before coming to a decision that is entirely their own, be it right or be it wrong.

Here's to those who accept they are different and revel in it, who enjoy standing out in the crowd, who know that they are unique and wonderful individuals but no more unique and wonderful than any other individual. Here's to those who nobody loves, those who society has cast out to sleep in the street as though they were nothing more than human garbage. Here's to those who won't accept authority and see it for what it is; an attempt by flawed, sick and dangerous people to gain power and control over others so that they can satiate their own perverse desires.

Here's to those who are appalled by the brutality we inflict on animals and weep at the way we rape the world that sustains us. Here's to those who feel outrage that 1% of humanity controls as much wealth as the other 99% does collectively, who are disgusted that even a single child should starve to death in a world of plenty. Here's to those who have principles and beliefs and who stick to them even when there's a price to be paid for doing so. Here's to those who have strange ideas and say stuff that they shouldn't say, who say "maybe things are not all they seem to be" and who carry on saying it even when others are laughing in their face. Here's to the gentle, the kind, the loving, the caring; here's to the meek and to the day when they shall inherit the Earth.

Here's to the old man standing on a street corner, protesting at the way things are, waving his walking stick in the air and shouting incoherently at passing traffic. Here's to the different, the strange, the eccentric, the odd, the looked down upon, the ignored, the outcasts, that funny bloke from number 37. Here's to the freaks. Here's to the future.

The Man Who Killed The Last Unicorn

Once upon a time...in the land of Anywhere, in a world long since forgotten, in the fine and prosperous city of Anyplace there lived a Banker. Despite being a rich and seemingly successful individual he was neither particularly bright nor talented – like all his kind he owed his wealth and position to The Magick Of The Old School Tie, a thuggish, brutish (even psychopathic) nature and the easy gains to be made once one was plugged into a Financialised Economic System that owned The Politicians and The Means Of Communication and was blatantly criminal in its nature; that kept all profits to itself but ensured that The Ordinary Folk compensated it for its losses.

In truth, The Banker was a thoroughly unpleasant sort. One of the things he enjoyed doing most, besides Rigging Financial Markets to enrich himself and destroy the lives of others, was hunting. He loved to dress himself up in the latest style of Aristocratic Idiot hunting gear and stroll pompously through the wild countryside surrounding the city of Anyplace, various guides, scouts and gillies In Attendance, killing as many animals as possible. For no other reason than entertainment and the satisfaction of his gross appetites. Oh, and to validate himself as a man for he was, in reality, so inadequate as one that only killing things made him feel like a Proper Person.

One day, on one of those hunts The Banker enjoyed so much, he wondered somewhat Off The Beaten Track, away from those

In Attendance, and found himself alone, forcing his way through an area of low, dense scrub and towering trees. He found that being alone actually made him feel More Of A Man and his excitement at the prospect of killing some poor animal became even more intense. That excitement grew markedly when he found himself in a clearing amongst the trees and scrub and saw, just ahead, unaware of his presence, chewing on a clump of lush grass – a Unicorn! The beautiful, extraordinary, almost mythical Unicorn. The ultimate hunter's trophy!

And therein lays our tale. For this Unicorn, chewing away peacefully on a clump of God's Green Grass in front of our vile Banker, was The Last Unicorn. The only one left in existence after widespread depredation and pollution of the Natural Environment by The Greedy One Percent and constant hunting by them and their Minions. To kill this one, fine and beautiful animal would permanently unstitch one of the Threads Of Creation from the Cloth Of The Universe. If The Banker had known this, would it have made any difference to his intention and desire to kill the animal? No, indeed it would have made the kill all the sweeter. Would it have made any difference to him if he had known that the act of removing A Thing Of Beauty forever from the fabric of the Universe would curse his Soul? No, for he would have thought that but a small problem that could be dealt with as any problem is dealt with – with money.

Oblivious of all the matters we have just discussed (for he was oblivious to all except money, power and self-gratification), The Banker raised his rifle to his shoulder and placed the Unicorn in his sights. But just as he was about to pull back the trigger and let fly a slug of hot, fatal metal - up popped a Faerie! As Faeries are wont to do in such circumstances.

Don't ask me where the Faerie had been, or where she had come from. I've no idea. Nobody knows how Faeries materialise and dematerialise at crucial and significant times, except perhaps because they are drawn to strong emotion like bees to honey – beyond that, it's impossible to explain, simply part of Faerie Magick, beyond the experience or knowledge of men. What I can say for sure is that the Faerie had materialised at this point and space in time to prevent a Gross Crime Against The Universe. It had determined that the last Unicorn was in danger of being killed and had decided it had to try to stop this awful event from occurring.

To this end, the Faerie materialised, with a pop and a bang, directly in front of the barrel of The Banker's gun. Flapping her diaphanous but powerful little wings she held a tiny hand, palm facing forward, to The Banker and said, 'stop, you cannot kill this Unicorn – it is the last of its kind and its death would be a Grievous Affront to the Universe!'

Now at this point, The Banker showed himself to be truly an ignorant man who knew everything of the ways of the world but nothing about the way the world worked. He should have realised that you never mess with a Faerie and if they tell you directly to something, you do it. He should have said, 'yes, Faerie' and 'of course, Faerie', instead he said:

'Hah, get out the way, Faerie, who are you to tell me what to do? This animal is mine, I shall have its head on my wall!'

'Do you not understand,' replied the Faerie, somewhat puzzled by this man's stupidity, 'this is the *last* Unicorn – if you remove a thing of such beauty from the Universe your Soul will be damned?'

'Oh shut up, Faerie, with your stupid talk of Souls and damnation...this is no longer your world and your so-called Magick has no power, your time has passed - the power of the age is money for money overcomes anything and I am a Man Of Money so your mumblings mean nothing to me!'

'Look,' said the Faerie, trying one more time to do the best for all concerned, 'it seems to me that Man Of Money you may be but man of sense, knowledge and wisdom you most definitely are not...do not do this, the consequences of your actions will be dire! I cannot stop you doing it, only try and persuade you, for I have to respect the Universal Law of Free Will, but if you do it do it, I warn you...I will bite you!'

At this point any sensible person would have turned heel and run, for to be bitten by a Faerie is to be cursed by a Faerie. Faerie Bites never, ever end well. But instead The Banker laughed, 'ha, ha...is that it? Is that the sum total of your pathetic power...you'll bite me! Why you are tiny and such a bite would be no more consequential than a gnat bit to me!'

'Anyway...you said it yourself, you cannot stop me...'

'But I beg you...please don't...'

'You cannot stop me, can you, Faerie?'

'No, regretfully, no...'

'Well then!'

And with that The Banker shoved the Faerie violently out of the way with the barrel of his gun and pulled the trigger. Gas exploded and expanded hugely and rapidly behind cold, hard metal and a super-charged slug of death sped through the air, taking the life of the Unicorn but milliseconds later. And a creature of such grace and beauty that it would become a thing of myth in not just one but many worlds, was Taken From Existence forever and we all became the poorer for it.

Seeing the Unicorn fall dead to the ground, The Banker jumped up and down, ecstatic, waving his gun above his head – not remotely upset that he had just removed a Thing Of Beauty from the Fabric of the Universe forever, just delighted that he'd killed something –even better, something so rare, the last of its kind, even!

The Faerie meanwhile observed events with despair and as the Unicorn died she shed a single Faerie tear of sadness, which turned into a diamond as it rolled down her cheek (as Faerie tears do) and dropped to the ground, its Shining Beauty lost forever in the dirt. But her job here was not yet done. In the blink of an eye she flew at The Banker, planting a Faerie bite in the middle of his forehead, just below his hairline. And then off she went - dematerialising and popping up at another intersection of time and space, deeply regretful that she had failed in her attempt to save the Unicorn but confident that the correct punishment had been meted out for such a heinous act.

The Banker was aware of none of this, he feared no Faerie and he feared no punishment, he was too rich to be punished after all! Attracted by his cries of jubilation, those In Attendance soon found him. He instructed them to take the Unicorn's head and have it stuffed and mounted. So happy was he that he decided to forgo returning to his wife and children in his palatial mansion in the hills outside of Anyplace, instead he would go to his townhouse in the city and treat himself to a whore to celebrate his fabulously successful hunt!

He was vaguely aware of a slight itching and a smudge of blood in the centre of his forehead, just below the hairline but gave it no import. It was surely nothing more than a Silly Little Gnat Bite.

The Banker proceeded with his plans. He went to his townhouse (in one of the most elegant and upmarket districts of Anyplace) and had the whore he'd promised himself. After the sex act had taken place, rather than pay the woman for services rendered, he beat her up and threw her out into the street. The Banker, and his kind, cannot approach any transaction fairly; they always, always have to make on Both Ends Of The Deal.

Later that night The Banker was lying asleep in his big, comfortable bed in his big comfortable house. He was dreaming happily about money and killing things. Were there any more species on the edge of extinction that he could kill? Suddenly he was awoken from his pleasant dream musings by an irritating itch in the centre of his forehead, just below the hairline. Humph, that damn gnat bite! he thought. He was also aware that he was feeling nauseous and feverish, in fact he was sweating buckets; he put a hand up to his forehead to examine the source of the annoying itching to find that what had been a tiny bite had swelled to the size of an egg! What was this? What was going on?

The Banker decided that he should get up out of bed, look at this strange growth in the mirror...

'Your soul will be damned...'

'I'll bite you...'

The Faeire's words ran around a dimly lit, rarely used corner of his mind and rose up into his consciousness, a little bubble of terror popping open – sudden realisation that a Faerie Bite was a Faerie Curse. Damn, perhaps he should have listened to the annoying Faerie...not killed the Unicorn...but, no, no, the thing on his forehead was but a bump. Maybe a septic gnat bite, nothing more, he was a man of Money, a man of Power, he had nothing to fear either from a bite gone bad or stupid Faeries spouting arcane nonsense about bites, curses and damnation! Hah! This is the Modern World, a world of Money not Magick!

Reassured, by his sensible, logical thoughts The Banker made to get up from his bed, have a look at the strange bump on his forehead and put some antiseptic on it. But he found he couldn't. He simply couldn't persuade his body to move. For not only was he feverish and nauseous he also weak, incredibly weak, his body simply wouldn't do what his mind wanted it to do. The irritation from the thing on his forehead reached a new pitch – what had just been itching was now a dull, painful throbbing. With effort, for he seemed to be getting weaker with every passing second, he lifted hand to forehead and examined the bump again. It was now even bigger! Warm. Throbbing. Painful. Malicious. Vengeful. Just under the surface of the bump he could feel something very hard, very pointed. Now the bump became the source of not just pain but excruciating, eye-crossing pain. And it exploded open in a shower of blood that The Banker could feel and see splattering across the ceiling above him and settling down as a fine, red mist across his face and his big, comfortable bed. Something was growing out of the centre of his forehead, just below the hairline. Something hard, pointed with a curled pattern running from top to bottom, wider at the base than at the sharp, pointed tip.

Oh, no...

Please no...

Oh God, please, not that....

What was growing from The Banker's forehead was a horn. A Unicorn Horn. And even as The Banker touched the horn, it grew and grew and the Pain Of Growth was like a nail being hammered into his brain. He screamed and screamed in utter agony. He tried once more to move, to get out his bed and run, somewhere, anywhere; but his body now had even less strength than just minutes ago...his hand slumped away from the thing growing out of him and lay inert and useless on a fine, goose feather pillow. Now he could move only his eyes. He rolled them back, upwards and the horn growing up from his forehead came into his field of vision. And The Bankers worst fears were confirmed, it was undoubtedly and unmistakably a Unicorn's Horn.

The pain stopped. The horn ceased its growth and The Banker ceased his screams. Silence reigned. The Silence Of The Grave.

That silence lasted only seconds. Because The Banker heard a strange collection of noises. Breathing, something that resembled a heavy foot stamping on the floor and...neighing.

Like a horse.

Like a...Unicorn.

The Banker rolled his eyes towards the source of the strange noises and his heart filled with terror...for there, in his room, was the Unicorn he had Taken From The Universe. And The Unicorn was staring at The Banker with a look of sheer, pure, unadulterated, vengeful hatred.

The Banker's pitiful, terrified screaming began again, and The Unicorn began to glow with a cold, unearthly blue light, a glow taken up by the horn sprouting from The Bankers forehead And as well as glowing, the horn started to grow faster - and bigger. It grew and grew until it reached the ceiling of The Bankers bedroom, at which point it attained some kind of

Magickal Flexibilty. It whirled around and around above The Banker and then struck down with great speed and force, plunging its sharp point deep into his genitals with a crunching sound and a huge gout of blood. The Banker's screams reached a new intensity. The horn withdrew itself, tip covered in blood and torn flesh, from The Bankers genital area and reared up and back and, in a move as gentle and careful and precise as the previous one had been swift and brutal, it popped first one of his eyeballs and then the other.

The helpless, dying banker screamed and screamed and screamed and begged for a Mercy That Was Not Forthcoming. The horn reared and plunged again and again, now with great violence, peppering The Banker's body with horrific wounds until he died and his rotten Soul exited his body to slink down to Hell and that Special Place that The Devil keeps for his Special Children.

All this was watched by The Unicorn who now wore on his face, if a Unicorn can wear such, a look of Great Satisfaction. The Unicorn observed events until The Banker's life expired and returned to wherever it had been Magicked from. With The Unicorn's departure, the horn atop The Banker's head lost the ghostly life that had entered it, shrank back and stilled and solidified. But it was still a fine Unicorn Horn protruding from a Banker's head.

The Banker's body was not discovered for several days. No neighbours had heard his dying screams and alerted the authorities for the neighbouring properties (like most of the properties in that area of Anyplace) were empty, having been bought not to live in but for Investment Purposes by members of The Greedy One Percent looking for ways to launder their ill-gotten gains. Nor was anyone (including wife and children) in a hurry to report The Bankers absence from place of work or marital home. People feared the man, but did not like nor respect him; his absence was a source of relief, not concern.

When The Bankers horribly mutilated, rotting corpse was finally discovered no coherent explanation could be found for the large Unicorn Horn growing from the middle of his forehead, just below the hairline. The cause of death would be listed as 'Death By Magick'.

And the moral of this tale is: 'there really are more things in heaven and earth...than are dreamt of in your philosophy.' (With thanks to Mr. Shakespeare).

The Princess Must Die!

Once upon a time...many, many years ago in a world long since forgotten, there was a country called Anywhere. And in the land of Anywhere there was a fine and prosperous city called Anyplace and in this fine city there was a very, very wealthy man, a member of the Aristocracy and the Greedy One Percent.

As is the way with Aristocrats he was a deeply unpleasant man: he came from a long line of Stupid but Brutal and Cunning Sociopathic predecessors who had robbed, lied, cheated and murdered their way to great riches. Why, then would you expect him to be anything else but a Pig Of A Man? After all, stupidity, brutality and a lack of compassion and even Basic Social Skills are common to all Aristocrats; a result of the Gross Inbreeding of their Limited Blood Lines and a Political And Legal System and Macro-Economic Environment that allows them to easily hold on to their stolen money and possessions despite their extra-ordinary ineptitude.

Anyway, this man, let's call him from this point on The Aristocrat, had a younger sister who was as different from him as Chalk was from Cheese. You see, the sister's birth had been witnessed by a Faerie who had just happened to be passing through that particular time and space, doing her usual work of checking up on the Doings Of Humanity.

Whilst entranced by the Eternal Beauty And Miracle of a life continuing its cycle, the Faerie had been more than a bit disgusted by the stench of Corruption and Ignorance emanating from the Souls of the child's Extremely Ugly Parents... and looking into the Soul of the newly-born child she was saddened to see that the girl would grow to be an adult like the parents: she would become an Ugly woman, bereft of Intelligence, Grace and Care.

Feeling desperately sorry for the girl, she cast a Faerie spell that would ensure the child would, instead, grow up with all the qualities so missing from her parents, and crossed her wings that her spell would not turn out to be too double-edged (as Faerie spells can sometimes be...).

And so it was that the Faerie spell came to pass. The Child reached adulthood as a Beautiful and Intelligent young woman, so unlike other female Aristocrats with their podgy, shapeless bodies, buck teeth, crossed-eyes, big ears, fat noses and inability to String A Simple Sentence Together. Even more strangely (for a member of the Aristocracy), she was a kind and compassionate woman and could even hold a conversation with the Ordinary Folk and relate to their lives and problems! Indeed, she spent much of her time with the Common People and became deeply involved with Charities And Organisations that were involved in their welfare.

Not surprisingly such a bright, attractive, intelligent and caring lady, a real and solitary jewel floating in the cesspool of Aristocracy, garnered much attention, soon becoming very popular with the Ordinary Folk and a darling of The Means Of Communication. From there, it was not long before this wildly liked and unusually attractive Aristocratic young lady was spotted by the Royal Family of the land of Anywhere. They decided that such a beautiful woman, so beloved by the Ordinary folk and The Means Of Communication, would make an ideal wife for their oldest son, The Prince, who being dense and strange even by Royal standards, needed a good marriage to improve his profile and standing with the Ordinary Folk.

And so, quicker than a Troll can run, the marriage was arranged. Truth be told, our sweet young lady, who we shall now have to call The Princess, did not want to marry The Prince; she considered him an unpleasant and ignorant man with very strange ideas and poor personal hygiene. But, being a Good Girl with a strong Sense Of Duty, she did as her family bade and married the strange and dysfunctional Prince.

Alas, the marriage was not to be a happy one. If the Prince and Princess had been buildings he would have been a claustrophobic, grey Mausoleum housing the dead whilst she would have been a Dance Hall full of light and music. Both partners soon grew apart, for they had absolutely nothing in common. The Prince took an older, less attractive and far more stupid lover, with whom he felt more comfortable, whilst The Princess threw herself even more into her Charitable Works and even began to campaign for better treatment of, and land rights for, the Troll Community! She, too, took a lover and many years later it would be revealed that of the two children the marriage produced one was, in fact, not fathered by The Prince but by a dashing Army Officer: to give you a clue as to which child that was I shall only say it was not the ugly and stupid one but rather the better looking and more interesting one.

Eventually it became difficult to hide from The Means Of Communication and the Ordinary Folk how unhappy the Prince and Princess were and this, together with the fact that the Princess had become even more popular and was totally eclipsing her miserable husband in the eyes of all, became a source of great embarrassment to the Royal Family. Not to mention her campaigning for land rights for Trolls...that being in direct challenge to the interests of the Banker Class who covet Troll land for Lucrative Re-development Purposes. Unacceptable!

It was decided that Princess had become a problem about which Something Had To Be Done. Putting their almost empty heads together to Collectively Utilise their limited intellect the Royal Family and their Greedy One Percent advisors (who actually did all the thinking) hit upon a solution. One which had always worked for their type in the past.

The Princess had to be killed.

And so it was that Orders Were Issued to Shadowy Government Departments and, in an operation overseen by the Evil Politician, Mass Murderer and War Criminal, Bonty Liar, the Princess was Tragically Killed in a Sad And Freak Accident.

Following the Princess's death there was a howling of outraged pain from the Ordinary Folk and criticism by them of The Royal Family for the Ordinary Folk felt that The Royals, who were simply acting in their usual dead-eyed, soulless way to the pain of others, were not showing much sadness at the passing of such a Beloved lady (in truth, The Royals were cock-a-hoop that this troublesome Princess was dead but the Common People were, of course, not aware of that).

Indeed, dis-satisfaction with The Royals reached such a clamour that a call went out from The Powers That Be to the tame Means Of Communication and the Owned Political Class to Co-Opt The Pain of the Ordinary Folk and save the reputation of The Royal Family.

Various Royal Idiots were wheeled out (sometimes literally) to express their sadness at the death of the Princess, even The

Prince was made to stand up and read a speech (written for him and transcribed in phonetics so that he would be able to, semi-intelligibly, speak what he saw) about his love for the Princess and how much he missed her. The Means Of Communication communicated on a twenty-four hour a day basis, day in day out how Dreadfully Missed was The Princess, how loved she had been by all, particularly by her husband and The Royal Family.

This Process Of Propaganda worked (as propaganda is wont to do) and soon The Reputation Of The Royals Was Rehabilitated

To fully placate The Ordinary Folk a lavish State Funeral was held for The Princess. At the funeral many Artfully Empty tributes were paid to The Princess by equally Artfully Empty people.

And at this point, I bring back into my little Tale the Princess's brother - The Aristocrat, he who was a Pig Of A Man. For he, too, gave a speech at The Princess's funeral. He stood up and talked about his sister in gushing and entirely false terms (actually he had accepted a very large sum of money from The Royals to supply intimate personal details about The Princess that were of vital use in planning her murder, but what else would you expect from one of his class?) speaking of his deep "love" and "respect" for her. He then announced that, as her brother, he would be Custodian of Her Body and Her Memory. He would build a fine mausoleum for The Princess in which her body would lie permanently In State on an island in the middle of a lake on one of his estates. For a small fee, The Ordinary Folk would be allowed to cross the bridge to the island and visit the mausoleum (The Aristocracy will always try to make money in any way they can, no matter how gross or crass).

There was one other attendee at the funeral that day. Unbidden and unknown, fluttering quietly away high above The Princess's coffin, was the same Faerie that had bestowed a spell upon The Princess at her birth. She had kept a keen eye on The Princess over the years and had been very proud of the way she had Turned Out, had come to love her for her Grace, Humanity and Humility. Her Princess had been a proper person and not a Piece Of Filth like the rest of her Loathsome Family or, even worse, the Family Of Monsters she had married into. The Faerie was, then, understandably distressed by events, more so because she had Faerie Insight of the disgusting Plottings And Machinations that had gone into murdering The Princess, a barbarity that even her own brother, the Pig Of A Man, had been party to.

Upon hearing The Aristocrat's plan to bury his sister's body on an island and charge admission she was less than amused and resolved that this was something that was simply Not Going To Happen. And with that, off she flew to consort with some friendly Trolls who owed her a favour or two.

By and by, the money-grubbing Aristocrat built his tasteless (and very cheaply done) mausoleum and installed his sister's body there. But the mausoleum was to be a very short-lived business venture, for the night before it was due to open to Paying Customers, it was tragically (at least to The Aristocrat who mourned the loss of a Potentially Lucrative Income Stream) attacked and utterly destroyed by a mass Troll Depridation. Even worse, said Evil Trolls stole the body of The Princess, no doubt to use for Nefarious Purposes.

This incident was presented by The Means Of Communication (faithful servant as ever to the Bankers) as yet another example of the Vileness Of Trolls, yet another reason to never trust The Other and the Wickedness Of Those Who Are Not Understood.

In fact there was, of course, nothing wicked in what the Trolls had done. They had been doing as our Faerie had requested of them, the aim being to give The Princess the Peace And Dignity in death that she had been denied in life: and the Trolls had done it gladly for The Princess, being one of the few humans to ever speak in their favour, had been much Loved and Respected in the Troll community.

Following the Faerie's instructions, the band of Trolls carried her body far into the wild countryside of Anywhere, climbing a high hill until they reached a beautiful, green and windswept plateau.

Here on this plateau they were met by a Mass Convocation Of Faeries and a huge crowd of Trolls, all having gathered to give The Princess a Proper Burial. The Convocation of Faeries hummed the Rhythm Of Life, a Faerie song (or humming, rather, for Faeries cannot sing) as old as time itself, and the Princess's body was born into the centre of the huge crowd of Trolls, where it was lain to rest on the richly scented soil from which it had originally sprung. From within the crowd of Trolls appeared four breathtakingly beautiful, blindingly white Unicorns, each with a fine, black horn. Using these fine horns (horns wrought by Magick) and their powerful hooves, they dug a deep trench into which was placed The Princess's body.

One by one, the huge crowd of Trolls passed by The Princess's new resting place, each picking up and casting into the grave a handful of rich, loamy soil. Two senior Trolls, old and wise in a way beyond any Human Experience, even paid to The Princess the ultimate display of Troll respect for the dead; each cutting off the little finger of his left hand and placing it in the grave with the body.

Soon The Princess's grave was filled with earth and the crowd of Trolls dispersed, back to their Troll Holes, but still the Convocation Of Faeries remained in the air above the grave, still humming the Rhythm Of Life. One Faerie, our Faerie, broke from the Convocation, flew downward and set herself upon the grave. In one last gesture, after which the Convocation would melt away, she said goodbye to the girl she had loved, cried one final Faerie tear, which (as Faerie tears do) turned into a diamond as it fell from her eye. The Faerie begged forgiveness from the Princess for the unintended Duality of the spell she had cast at her birth and sowed the earth of the grave with an enchanted mix of plant seed, seed of beautiful and richly scented flowers which would grow and blossom every single day of the year, be it winter, summer or anywhere in between, until the very Stars Fell From The Sky.

Don't Sleep!

Don't sleep. Because life is short and if you blink, you'll miss it.

Don't sleep. Because you never know when life will end.

Don't sleep. Because if you do regret will haunt you.

Don't sleep. Because there's no second time around the merry-go-round; this really is not a rehearsal.

Don't sleep. Because this world holds more than enough magic and wonder for one hundred lives let alone just one.

Don't sleep. Because there's far more stuff that you don't know than there is stuff that you do know.

Don't sleep. Because you've got a hell of a lot to learn if you're ever going to be the person you were meant to be.

Don't sleep. Because if you do you'll never get done all the things you were put here to get done.

Don't sleep. Because if you do I can't even begin to tell you how much great stuff you're going to miss.

Don't sleep. Because where's the fun in not taking part?

Don't sleep. Because there is always a new passion, a new friend, a new challenge.

Don't sleep. Because your youth is a depreciating asset, going rapidly out of fashion.

Don't sleep. Because there is sex and dancing and music.

Don't sleep. Because you have a body, enjoy its senses and its potential - use it!

Don't sleep. Because you have more gifts than you know.

Don't sleep. Because even when life is at its blackest change for the better can come at any time, usually when you least expect it.

Don't sleep. Because through your veins flows the power of a thousand suns.

Don't sleep. Because the odds of you been being born as you were actually infinitesimal, but still you did it.

Don't sleep. Because despite all the pain and disappointment and flotsam and jetsam and layers of lies and deception, it really, really is a beautiful world (trust me on that one).

Don't sleep. Because, as they say, you're a long time dead.

The Unsuitable Suitor

Once upon a time...many, many years ago in a world long since forgotten, there was a country called Anywhere. And in the land of Anywhere there was a fine and prosperous city called Anyplace and this city was home to a charming Young Couple. The couple were not yet Married or Living in Sin (for this was as common in the land of Anywhere as it is in your own time and place), rather they were Walking Out with a view to Getting Married.

It was agreed by the people of the neighbourhood that the Young Couple were indeed a very handsome pair who seemed very happy together, Much In Love and, oh, what beautiful children they would have!

So, all was well with this charming Young Couple. Until...

Until Class And Money raised their ugly heads.

You see, there was a considerable difference in the Social Standing of each half of this particular lovely Young Couple. The Boy, whom we shall know as Frederick, was of humble origins, for his parents were farmers. He himself had come to the city of Anyplace at the age of eighteen to pursue his love of Painting, which it was generally agreed he was really rather good at. One day, maybe, he would be a Rich And Famous Painter. But maybe not, for few of those Equally Blessed And Cursed with an Artistic Temperament learn to Monetise Its Value.

At least that was the way the parents of The Girl, whom we shall know as Isobel, thought.

Isobel's parents were Concerned Parents who considered themselves to have their daughter's Best Interests At Heart. They did not approve of Isobel's relationship with Frederick, for the boy's Chosen Occupation and Humble Background simply were not good enough, he was an Unsuitable Suitor. Isobel's parents were Wealthy And Successful merchants who had made a fortune trading and selling insurance against Troll attacks: Troll Depredation Insurance as it was known in the land of Anywhere. They considered it entirely realistic that within a decade or so, given more hard work on their part and a Good Marriage on Isobel's, their family could join the ranks of the Truly And Extraordinarily Wealthy One Percent and live in one of the Fine Mansions in the hills outside Anyplace.

For this reason, they decided that Isobel's romance with Frederick had to come to an end. The parents had believed that Isobel would grow out of Her Infatuation with the boy, but over a year had passed now since the two had met and still that had not happened. The girl obviously needed a Talking To; she had to be made to see The Error of Her Ways.

And so the Concerned Parents sat Isobel down and explained to her The Way Of The World. They explained to her that her boyfriend, though very handsome and talented in an Artistic Way, was, given his chosen career path, unlikely ever to have Real Money. Who then would buy her all the Gorgeous Dresses And Shoes, from the Chicest Shops in Anyplace, that she was so fond of? And the Jewellery? And the Exotic Perfumes? And where would she live? Did she really want to live her life in Frederick's poky little rented flat in a Poor Area of the city? And imagine, if they should have children, there would be no money for a nanny and she would have to raise them herself!

Oh, the indignity of it all! How her friends would Laugh At Her!

Isobel sat there quietly and listened to her parents, considering her response. And at this point I know you want me to say that Isobel weighed her Love for Frederick against all the Shallow And Petty Concerns that her parents had raised and came down Firmly On The Side Of Love. I'm afraid not. For Isobel was truly her parents' daughter. At the root of her being, she *was* shallow and she *was* obsessed with money and position. She concluded her parents were right. Frederick had to go; he really was an Unsuitable Suitor. She had to make a Good Marriage. That way she would get all the Good Things In Life that she so deserved, that she was Entitled To.

The very next day she sent one of her father's servants to the lowly area of Anyplace where Frederick lived to deliver him a Letter. In the Letter, she told Fredrick that she did not love him and never had, he had been but a Diversion that had Run Its Course and she no longer wanted to see him or even to know him.

Poor Frederick was heart-broken. He knew he and Isobel had indeed loved each other. Why had this happened? To be so curtly and brutally dismissed. He did not understand.

Lovelorn and lost, Frederick took to waiting outside the house where Isobel lived. He would wait until she left the property and follow her around the city. He did not do this to stress or distress her, for Frederick was a Truly Good Man with nothing but Love in his Soul; rather he did it because he still loved her intensely, despite her Cruel Rejection. Even to see her from afar filled his heart with joy.

Unfortunately, Frederick's Sad And Lost Behaviour did not go unnoticed. In fact his following of Isobel's every footstep became the Subject Of Gossip. When this Gossip reached the ears of Isobel's father he was Deeply Disturbed and Apoplectically Angry. Fearing that such idle chatter might damage his daughter's chances of making a Good Marriage, he decided that Something Had To Be Done.

Now, Isobel's father had, as do all wealthy people, a Dark Little Secret. You see, the market in Troll Depredation Insurance in the land of Anywhere is fuelled by the on-going and continuous nature of Troll attacks and general Troll-related mischief. Unknown to the public, though, the majority of said Troll attacks were instigated and paid for by Isobel's father to keep demand for his insurance services buoyant. This was a vital constituent of his business's Marketing Strategy and was a necessary one for, in reality, Trolls are Peaceful creatures who have been stigmatised by humans for being The Other and because Bankers covet Troll land for Development Purposes.

Having paid for so many Troll attacks over the years, Isobel's father had Extensive Contacts within the Troll community and decided to use these to "warn off" Frederick once and for all.

One night, a particularly large and reluctantly aggressive Troll (with a hefty payment from Isobel's father stashed safely away back at his Troll hole) sneaked into the city of Anyplace under Cover Of Darkness. Stealthily, the Troll made his way to Frederick's small flat. Skilfully and quietly he broke in, found his way into Frederick's bedroom and bundled the hapless fellow into a Large Sack he had bought with him for just such a purpose.

Throwing the sack, kicking and screaming Frederick and all, over one burly shoulder, the Troll made his way back out of Frederick's flat and ran through the streets of Anyplace at that incredible speed that can be attained by a Troll in a hurry, that being slightly faster than the animal that you know in your world as a cheetah.

Soon the Troll and Frederick were outside the City Limits, the Troll still running. A few minutes later and Frederick and his kidnapper were deep within an isolated patch of forest.

The Troll stopped. He dropped the sack from his shoulder and shook it until Unfortunate Fredrick fell out. Then taking a hammer and a sharp knife, before the Dazed And Confused Frederik had time to react, he sliced deep cuts up and down the poor man's face and used the hammer to break every finger on both of his hands.

Bewildered, shocked and in deep pain Frederick lay there in the dirt of the forest floor still unsure as to what had just happened. Then all became clear. As Frederick lay crying and bleeding, the Troll crouched down next to him and told him to stay away from Isobel: if he did not then he and Frederick would meet again and that meeting would make this one seem like a Cosy Chat between friends.

Standing up, the Troll threw his head back and gave a long, loud and evil laugh (more for effect than anything else as Troll's are very given to the Dramatic Gesture) before sprinting away. As he ran back to his Troll hole, the Troll, in reality, felt very sorry for Frederick. He had only done what he had done for money, for like all his kind he had been forced, by the Machinations And Greed of the Bankers, into abject poverty and desperation: he had a brood of Trollettes to feed back at his

Troll hole, and if he had to commit violence to keep them fed and healthy then so, reluctantly, be it.

Frederick was left there, in the dirt, mud and leaves, sliding in and out of consciousness, slowly bleeding to death from the wounds on his face, for the Troll (Trolls being notorious for not knowing their own strength) in his attack had unknowingly cut far too deeply, turning what should have been a warning into a Potentially Fatal Occurrence.

And bleed to death he would have done if at that exact point had not Fate, the Blind Old Weaver who spins together the Threads of Our Lives, randomly spun together some Good Fortune. For along came a Faerie.

Now, in the land of Anywhere, Fairies are pretty much universally feared. This is for two reasons. The first is that they can see deep into the Human Soul and divine a person's nature in seconds. You can hide nothing from a Faerie. The second reason is the Duality Of Their Nature. Fairies are capable of using their Not Inconsiderable Powers Of Magic for Great Good but, unfortunately, Fairies also have a naturally Mischievous Nature and knowing exactly how Faerie magic might turn out in any given situation is nigh on impossible! For these reason, then, it is needless to say that people in the land of Anywhere try to avoid Fairies at all costs.

So how would this Unpredictable-By-Nature little Faerie creature choose to react to poor, injured Frederick?

Fortunately for Frederick, this particular Faerie had a Story. What you would not know in your world is that Fairies live for precisely 897 years and 13 days. And then, they simply Dematerialise and cease to exist. Now on that particular day, our particular Faerie had reached the exact half-way point in her 897 years and 13 days of existence. This had caused her to reflect that so far in her life she had been quite a Tinkerously Mischievous Faerie and, to not mince words, whilst she had never used her powers to do anything Really, Really Bad, nor had she done anything Really, Really Good.

But staring down at Frederick, now completely unconscious, the Faerie examined his Soul and saw that there was nothing bad there, he was a Truly Good Man who was full of only Love and Beauty, a man who was a painter and a True Artist, and she was moved: she could help this Good Man, and finally do an Entirely And Unequivocally Good Thing in her life. In doing so she could not only Redeem herself but also pay tribute to the Beloved Memory of her Faerie life-partner who had reached her 897th year and 13th day just the year before (it is a common feature of Faerie Partnerships that one partner is usually much older than the other) and who had been, in all ways possible, a very, very Good Faerie.

Seeking Her Redemption, the Faerie hovered above Frederick, closed her eyes, spread her arms and opened her mouth, from which came a low humming noise followed by a cloud of glittering, golden dust which gathered around the Faerie's head before streaming off in two directions, half of the dust cloud coating Frederick's bleeding face, the other half his broken fingers. The wounds glittered and shone, the Faerie closed her mouth and opened her eyes, the dust disappeared and Frederick's wounds were healed: his face was scarred and still mutilated but no longer bleeding: his fingers were knobbly and twisted and deformed, but no longer broken.

Frederick would not now die of his wounds, but the Faerie was aware that there were limits to her restorative powers.

Frederick would no longer be a handsome man; indeed his face would be something that, on dark nights, would scare Small Children. And his hands. His battered hands! He would never paint again. So the Faerie decided to give this Good Man one more Gift. From this day on, as long as Frederick held a paintbrush in his hands, Faerie Magick would do the rest and he would be able to commit to canvas the beauty that was in his Soul. As a final touch, just because she couldn't completely deny her nature, much as she might try or might want to, and had to slip a bit of mischievousness in there somewhere, Frederick would only be able to paint the Beauty of His Soul for as long as he remained a Truly Good Man.

Her job done and feeling very Righteous, the Faerie went on her way. Now she had done something good she could spend her final days being especially naughty: she was off to inflict some Universal Justice on some bad and maybe steal a human child or two (actually Faeries steal human children for entirely positive reasons but you can read about that in the next story). What fun she was going to have!

Eventually Frederick awoke and found his way out of the forest. Back at his humble home he sat down and cried. What had happened to him? He remembered the Troll's warning and the savage attack. But after that? How had his wounds healed so quickly? Somebody must have helped, but who? And why had they bothered? He had lost so much. He knew he could never see Isobel again, not just because the Troll would kill him but also because what woman would be interested in a man with such a Hideously Scarred face? Just as bad, Frederick realised, looking at his twisted fingers, that he'd never paint again. What was the point in living?

For some days Frederick lay in his bed trying to die but, frustratingly, unable to do so.

Then one particular and blessed day, his gloom seemed to lift and he was suddenly possessed of an Over-Powering And Irresistible urge to paint. But surely that was ridiculous? What could he do with his crippled fingers?

Nevertheless, not many breaths later, Frederick found himself in front of a Blank Canvas and a Selection Of Paints. Awkwardly, he clasped a paint brush and gasped in amazement as his hand and arm took on a life of their own, painting a picture Unbidden And Unaided. He passed into a calm and warm trance, awaking only when the picture was finished. And what a picture it turned out to be! It was completely abstract in nature, shot through with beautiful colour and shapes that pleased and enticed the eye, soothed the mind and raised the spirits.

Frederick saw he had just done something no artist had done before. He had created a picture of the Beauty In His Soul.

From that day Frederick would carry on painting and after a number of years was Immensely Rich And Well-Regarded, his paintings being seen as things of True Beauty, Much in Demand and Highly Valuable. And despite his physical shortcomings and loss of his Beloved Isobel (Frederick never married, never able to free himself of the memory of his One And Only, All-Encompassing True Love), he became Happy With His Life and would eventually move into a fine house in the Best Part Of Town becoming, as well as Very Rich, a Noted Society Figure.

Meanwhile, things had gone badly for Isobel. Her family's business had collapsed when a member of one of the families of the One Percent had spotted the Untapped Potential in Troll

Depredation Insurance and had started up a Highly Geared Business that squeezed Isobel's family out of the market with Predatory Pricing and Cross Subsidy.

The family's wealth vanished like Faerie Mist on a summer's morning and Isobel's parents had to throw themselves upon the Government and move into Social Housing. Upon finding out that Isobel was no longer wealthy, all her Fine Friends deserted her and her husband (who had turned out to not be such a good catch after all) threw her and their two children out into the street and had the doors to his Fine Home barred against them. He didn't want a Pauper for a wife and certainly was not ready to support her Mewling Brats.

Seeking Shelter for herself and the children, the Devastated Isobel went to her parents' dilapidated Government tenement down a dark and dirty ginnel. They decided they had more than enough of their own problems and told her and her whining children to seek shelter elsewhere.

Desperate, Isobel could think of only one other place to go. To the home of a man who was now a Rich And Famous Artist: a man she had once loved, a man who, in her heart of hearts, she still loved. A man who perhaps still loved her.

And so Isobel appeared on Frederick's doorstep.

Upon opening his door and seeing Isobel there, Frederick found himself lost for words, as all his old feelings of love for her came flooding back. She explained her circumstances to him, begged his forgiveness for the way she had treated him and appealed for help, if not for her then at least for the Children

At that point Frederick nearly, nearly, took Isobel back into his life. But then his Heart Hardened. He thought of the pain and physical damage she had, directly and indirectly, caused him.

He could not Forgive her. He just could not do it. Quietly he closed the door in her face and she and her Children slunk away to be lost in the dense Fog Of Forgotten Stories that makes up so much of history.

For a few moments, Frederick stood in the Grand Hallway of his Grand Home and thought that maybe, just maybe, he should have forgiven Isobel and taken her in? Perhaps, even at this late stage, they could have Built A Life Together? But no, she had been Too Cruel to him; he had done The Right Thing. Hadn't he? Or had he sacrificed his love for Isobel on the Altar of His Own Pride? Had he caused pain to Isobel and himself? Had a Good Man done a Bad Thing?

Later that night, Frederick decided to try and improve what had been a bad day by painting one of his Much Desired artworks. He sat in front of a blank canvas. As usual his hands and arms began their work and he lapsed into his familiar trance-like state. And then he awoke. And what was before him was a disaster. The canvas was black, just black, an expanse of flat, dead, emotionless, Meaningless Black paint. It was nothingness, bereft of Beauty And Soul. In a fit of panic, Frederick grabbed another blank canvas and tried again. The result was another dead mass of black. He tried again and again, working through the night but nothing changed and by the morning he had accumulated a collection of eight worthless, pointless, lifeless black canvases.

Frederick collapsed to the floor and sobs racked his body. He knew that he had made a bad decision, done the Wrong Thing and that something inside him had died; a thing of Great Beauty had left his life for ever, a Precious Gift - no, two Precious Gifts, had been taken away and would never be returned.

And the motto of this story is: if you're a good person, stay a good person – whatever life chooses to throw at you, stay good.

The Nature of Love (Anywhere and Everywhere)

Life...is a random, cacophonous noise full of screaming and shouting and things that glitter and shine but turn out to be not what they seem.

In all that distracting, attention-seeking noise there is only one indisputable constant: Love. For only Love has true and enduring value.

Success and wealth are fabulous, but they are relative and all too often transitory. And at the end of your story on this earth, when the Blind Old Weaver Of Fate is spinning together the final threads of your life, no matter how much success you've gained or how much "stuff" you've bought, they will not hold your hand and mop your brow as your Soul prepares to journey across a Broad, Bright, Blue Sky and your life slips inevitably into The Fog of Forgotten Stories. Only Love will hold you firm. Only Love will gather you up to itself and comfort you, whisper sweet words that calm your Soul and speed it on its final journey to That Which Lies Beyond.

Throughout your life and until The Very End, only love will weave that Shining Web Of Gossamer beneath you, to catch you should you fall.

So don't be distracted by the noise and the bling, by the things that shine so brightly and alluringly, by that which promises much but delivers little. Don't be tempted by regret, hatred and bitterness; they are harsh masters. Don't judge yourself, don't judge others, always walk that mile in another man's shoes. Be kind, be caring; always share and treasure a caress. Seek to leave behind no bad feeling but rather try to add to the Greater Sum of Happiness because everyone, not least yourself, deserves respect, dignity and a chance at life. Above all, remember that to live this life, and leave this world, having loved and having been loved is all that really matters. The rest ain't worth a damn.

The System

Once upon a time...many, many years ago in the land of Anywhere, in a world long since forgotten, there was, at one time, a kind of Golden Age. It was not, it has to be said, an age that was Perfect but it was agreed by almost all that it was an age that was much, much better than That Which Had Gone Before. That time is best described by quoting from a well-known article historical document contemporaneous to the period ...

'...after Generations Of Struggle against Social Injustice and two Catastrophic And Immensely Bloody Wars with the nearby land of Anotherplace, in which the Ordinary Folk had died and suffered to a catastrophic degree, it was decided by all except the Rapaciously Rich that Things Had To Change.

From that point on, Ordinary Folk were given access to Free Education, Free Healthcare, Pensions, Benefits to help those who fell upon Hard Times and all the advantages of what you would know in your world as a Welfare System. New taxes were introduced to redistribute some of the vast sums of money accumulated (mostly from Stealing, Cheating and Aggressive Tax Avoidance) by the Wealthy and the Aristocracy (known in the land of Anywhere as The Greedy One Percent) over the years and Political Reforms introduced to break their stranglehold over the Political And Economic Life of the country. Additionally, the Right to Vote was given to all.

And the land of Anywhere blossomed, for it was found that a populace Free From Hunger And Illness, that was properly Educated and Cared For, produced huge numbers of Talented men and women who previously had Languished due to Poverty And

Lack of Opportunity. These Talented men and women drove the land of Anywhere to new heights of success, founding businesses, employing people, making a mark in the worlds of politics, science, medicine and culture. Slowly but surely, the Dead Grip of The Greedy One Percent, who had dominated and controlled the land of Anywhere for as long as anyone could remember, was broken.'

And the psychopathic Greedy One Percent, the Devil's Children, hated this new world, this New Bargain and Better Society, and all it stood for. They vowed to destroy it.

So they invented The System - a political and economic way of running the economy and society that ensured that those who operated The System, that being The Greedy One Percent, would always getter richer and you, The Ordinary Folk, would always get poorer.

The System dressed itself up as democracy. But this was a lie. For, whenever, an election came round The System would invest time and energy into a Demographic Analysis of voters thoughts, opinions and aspirations, discerning and identifying from the Research distinct 'Voter Groups' and it would appoint one if its Puppet Politicians to be a candidate to represent each of these Voter Groups. The puppet assigned to each group would promise to deliver whatever it was that group was hoping for from the election (as previously deduced from the Research). Once elected, however, the chosen puppet would ignore the wishes of those who had elected him or her and act only in the interests of The Greedy One Percent (the puppet masters). Thus it was that The System ensured that whoever won an election, The System won the election.

And The System got away with this blatant fraud because it was ably supported by The Means Of Communication, which was, of course, owned by The Greedy One Percent. No lie was too blatant or obvious for The Means Of Communication, indeed it no longer functioned as anything that could be remotely called 'journalism', it was simply the propaganda mouthpiece of The System, churning out lies and distortions every hour of every day of every year; lies and distortions designed to manipulate The Ordinary Folks and hide the machinations of The Greedy One Percent.

And The System, supported by The Means Of Communication, was proficient not only at telling lies but also at creating whole stories to work to their advantage. These were called False Narratives; sophisticated and intricate lies, supported and disseminated not only by The Means Of Communication but also by Scientists and Not Government Operations (both supposedly independent but, in truth, reliant on The System for their position and funding). These stories, these False Narratives, could run over periods of many years and were designed to take the concern and good intentions of genuine people and lead them up Blind Allies. One of the most sophisticated False Narrative in the history of Anywhere was the Fighting Against Terrorism Narrative which claimed, on the basis of lies and exaggeration, that Terrorism was a Major Threat To Our Way Of Life that would require a generation long struggle to combat. It would require wars to be fought in Far Away Lands and Constant Vigilance. And the wars to be fought in foreign lands were fought in countries that had no connection to Terrorism but were rich in Natural Resources that The Greedy One Percent wished to plunder and steal for themselves. And the Constant Vigilance meant legislation to restrict the Civil Liberties of The Ordinary Folk and the creation of a Surveillance

State in which just disagreeing with The System would see you labelled as a peddler of Fake News, a Conspiracy Theorist and, of course, a Terrorist. The real truth that in the land of Anywhere, you were more likely to be killed by a lightning strike than an Act Of Terrorism.

And The System was also supported and ably abetted in its crimes by The Politicians. A loathsome class of people made up almost entirely of liars, charlatans, thieves, fraudsters and rapists. But The System did not care - for this was to its advantage, The Politicians bad habits made them easier to control; dark-hearted, empty-souled emissaries of The Greedy One Percent would visit members of The Political Class and say 'we know what you've done, do our bidding' or 'tell me, what's your desire – money, power, a fresh-faced child? Do our bidding and you shall have whatever you most want...' By these means The System controlled and used The Politicians to further its aims. The Politicians sent the children of The Ordinary Folk to die in unjust and illegal wars in far flung countries (not to further 'democracy' as The Politicians claimed – another False Narrative - but to rape and plunder the resources of other nations to make ugly and perverse, rich old men even richer). Furthermore, The Politicians also served The System by legislating to increase taxes on The Ordinary folk and cut them for the rich, to make the working lives of The Ordinary Folk ever more insecure, to spend more on arms and wars and less on education and health, to cut benefits and welfare. The Politicians also worked on behalf of The System to make easier the process of 'worldisation', by which process The Greedy One Percent exported the well-paid jobs of The Ordinary Folk to Slave Labour economies, and gave the Corporations owned by the same Greedy One Percent legal powers that meant they could overturn the decisions of governments, thus enabling their rape and plunder of the land's resources and destruction of the environment. And in many, many sundry ways not here described The Politician's worked for The System to make the lives of The Ordinary Folk harder and smaller.

And The System was most ably supported of all by The Financial System, led by The Banks (and guess who owned The Banks...) and The Bankers. Bankers, of course, are criminals of the most blatant and revolting kind who operate within criminal organisations that The Politicians declare legal by giving them the label of Banks. And The Bankers invented a new and wonderful Financial System, one so corrupt that it was primed to periodically explode under the weight of its own criminality. And each explosion would result in a financial crisis and The Bankers would cry 'give us money or the The Financial System will fail and there will be no food in the shops.' The Means Of Communication and The Politicians would support this ridiculous assertion (this False Narrative) and huge sums of money would be transferred from The Ordinary Folk to The Greedy One Percent and their Banks to be paid for by yet more taxes on The Ordinary Folk and yet more cuts in spending on welfare, health, education and anything else that might conceivably benefit the lives of The Ordinary Folk. The Financial System was nothing more than a means of transferring as much money as possible from The Ordinary Folk to the vastly wealthy...a system in which The Greedy One Percent got to keep all of the profits they made and got the taxpayer to compensate them to cover any losses they made. What was not to like!

And The System was best summed up by The Good Politician who, in his final speech to a crowd of thousands in The Park Of A Thousands Joyous Souls (just days before his strange and unexplained 'accidental death') described it thus:

"We are ruled by psychopaths. Our political and economic system is a giant criminal enterprise run by them for their benefit and their benefit alone. To them human life has no value, we are simply a commodity to be exploited, our sole function is to be consumers, tiny cogs in a huge, unsustainable machine that is powered by raping the planet. Our 'free press' is nothing but a peddler of propaganda and our democracy is a bought and paid for pantomime and a lie. Whoever wins, nothing ever changes. The Greedy One Percent always win for all candidates are their candidates. We are ruled by psychopaths, they are The Devil's Children and they are driving the world to destruction."

And the moral of this tale is: so, now you know about The System. The question is – what are you going to do about it?

Poor Man, Rich Man

Once upon a time in the land of Anywhere, in a world long since forgotten, in the fine and prosperous city of Anyplace, a Poor Man was walking to work. Now this man lived in a run-down flat in one of the deprived zones that encircle the bustling financial district of Anywhere, the City, and to get to his place of work (for he was employed in a nearby branch of McSlurry) he had to cross the thriving hub of finance.

So there he was, a Poor Man dressed in cheap clothes, strolling along the affluent pathways of this wealthy area. As he walked, he whistled, for the sun was bright and the sky was blue and there was happiness in his Soul.

Coming in the opposite direction, walking towards the Poor Man, was a Rich Man. He was a trader in the new financial product that had taken the City by storm in recent months, the HORFIOD (Highly Opaque and Risky Financial Instrument Of Death) and, as such, was a member of the families of The One Percent and lived, like the rest of his kind, in a fine house in one of the best parts of Anywhere.

Now today was not a good day for the Rich Man as he was particularly weighed down with the troubles and cares of wealth and was running frantically from business meeting to business meeting and he was not happy, not happy at all.

He was somewhat affronted, then, to see the Poor Man. After all, here was this chap coming down the street towards him, smiling, whistling and obviously in love with the world, yet from his demeanour and cheap clothes he was equally obviously a Poor Man of no means and no money. What right had he to be so offensively cheerful? What possible cause could he have to be so happy? Unacceptable! He determined that he would find out what was going on with this strange fellow, this insolent Poor Person

With this thought upon his mind and being by now in a very bad mood, the Rich Man, upon drawing level with the Poor Man said, "You, Poor Man, stop!"

And the Poor Man stopped, looked the Rich Man in the eye and, smiling in an infuriatingly pleasant way replied, "of course, sir, how may I help you?"

"Well, I'll come straight to the point. I found your obvious happiness an effrontery and most annoying and I wish you immediately to cease smiling and stop whistling. You have no right to be happy, I can tell simply from looking at you that you're a man without money and means and as such your position in life should be one of abject misery and I demand that you behave in a manner fitting and appropriate to your miserable station in life!"

"But, sir," replied the Poor Man, "respectful of your authority and all as I am, I have to beg to differ. You're right, of course, that money is a constant worry but I have a roof over my head and food on the table and a job of work. I have a wife who I love very much and who loves me and I have two beautiful, healthy children who are the apple of my eye...these things are Jewels Beyond Price."

"Jewels Beyond Price! Hah! What balderdash! Why, my fine house has twenty bedrooms and the largest of these is bigger, I'll wager, than the entire hovel in which you no doubt live."

"Then, sir, I'm sure you would win that bet for my home is humble indeed, but it is a happy home and that is enough for me"

"Ah, you fool! My wife is a former model and beautiful beyond compare, the kind of woman you most assuredly could not afford! Your own wife, I'm sure, is some fat, frumpy old fishwife and a pain to the eye."

"But, sir, I love my wife as my life itself, as she does me. Every time I look at her I see the most beautiful woman in the world and that is more than enough for me."

"What an idiot you are Poor Person! Why my children have the best of everything, they want for nothing, what do *your* mewling brats have?"

"Well, sir, it'd be true to say my children do not have as many...things...as yours but they are fed and clothed, loved and protected and encouraged in all they do and every night as I kiss them in their beds as they lay sleeping I see that they are smiling contentedly and that is certainly enough for me."

"Hah! What a pathetic Poor Fool you are, you understand nothing. I am a powerful and feared man, and what are you...I mean, look at you...who would ever fear you!"

"No, sir, I am not feared, nor would I want to be, I am happier having the good friends I have who like me for being me, not because they fear me."

"Moron! Fool! Imbecile! Look, let me put this in simple terms that even someone as impoverished and brainless as yourself would understand. I have *more* than you and this time next year I will have *even more* than you and the year after that I will have *more again* and the next year I will have *still more* than you and so on and so on until I have everything and you have nothing! There, now what do you say to that you scummy peasant!?"

"Sir, I can only say once again that I am blessed in what I do have, I do not like to waste my time worrying about what I do not have. Why would I want more when I already have enough?"

"Harrumph!" Harrumphed the Rich Man and, concluding, in sheer frustration, that there was no reasoning with this insolent fool of a man, span on his heel and walked away, leaving the Poor Man to continue his journey.

What a deluded idiot! Good grief! thought the Rich man. *'Why would I want more,' indeed! How stupid; after all, one always wants more, getting more is the point of everything. What kind of life can one have if one doesn't have more?* And yet...he could still hear that stubborn, insolent, stupid, *happy* Poor Man whistling as he walked away down the street. Happy? Nonsense! Love? Nonsense! Children? Nonsense! Happiness is money and then more money. Plain and simple.

But with that thought, something strange happened to the Rich Man. Maybe it happened because he was having a bad day, too much stress, too much to do, or maybe it happened because a mischievous and malignant Devil is always ready to sharply remind us of who we really are.

Whatever the cause, the Rich Man was suddenly struck by an intense bout of insight: something which people of his class and wealth are normally blissfully free of. He saw his life for what it was. His pretty, younger wife. Married not for love, but as a trophy. He didn't love her. And she didn't love him, not for a minute, his touch repulsed her. But she did love the money, the clothes, the parties, the house and the jewels. And as for the two children: they were far from being the apple of his eye. In fact he barely knew them, certainly didn't love them: they were just something that had to be produced by a man in his position; to his wife, giving birth to them was part of the financial contract that was their marriage. Raised by nannies and governesses, his children were growing up unloved and unwanted and would become troubled and difficult adults. And that big, beautiful house of his? Upon reflection it was big but not beautiful; rather, a cold, empty space devoid of meaning and feeling.

All he had was money. Lots and lots of money. But money can't share a joke or a confidence with you; it cannot be your friend. It cannot hold your hand, or kiss you or hold you near.

With this shock of insight the Rich Man suddenly felt very alone. He felt a sense of rising panic and anxiety, of sorrow and loss. He stopped walking. He felt hot and sick and dizzy and...and at that point his heart, weakened by years of stress and rich living, decided to give up the struggle and ceased to beat.

The Rich Man fell to the ground, aware of an absence of motion in his chest and an inability to breathe. This was it, he was dying! But this could not be, for surely he was Too Rich To Die?

And just before the Rich Man made the final journey from this world to the other, his insight suddenly widened further and he had a vision of the very inside of his Soul, and his last living feelings were ones of endless and deep despair. He saw his Soul for what it was: a vast, empty, barren desert in which there was not a living thing except a myriad rats, scuttling pointlessly and desperately back and forth in search of something they didn't even know they were looking for and would never find, and across the thick, black fur of each of these rats was emblazoned, in blood red capital letters, the word GREED.

At this point the Rich Man's existence slipped into the dense Fog Of Forgotten Stories which makes up so much of history and his Soul passed into the possession of He who had always really owned it – He who had bought it for the price of meaningless bling and shiny baubles of Earthly wealth - the Swallower of Souls, the Devil.

I hope you enjoyed my little tales...if you did you can read more
Tales from Anywhere in my book 'The Real Story of God and
The Devil' which is available to buy now...to further tempt you
here's part of a tale from that book...

Too Wicked For Hell

Once upon a time in the land of Anywhere, in a world long since
forgotten, in the fine and prosperous city of Anyplace there was
a politician, let's call him The Politician, who was a particularly
unpleasant example of this exceptionally low form of humanity.
He led a corrupt, self-serving and immensely destructive life and,
in a remarkable and unusual incident of justice, would eventually
end his existence swinging from the end of a rope after being
tried and convicted of war crimes and crimes against humanity.
And as his body swung lifelessly in the air, its soul exited the
Earthly Remains. Upon which event, highly specialised
computer systems somewhere in a far off, dusty corner of Heaven
(at the least those are the best terms I can think to describe
what happened, for the mechanics of Heavenly Bureaucracy are
beyond the whit and ken of mere mortals) sprang automatically
into action. The celestial and spiritual equivalent of bytes and
megabytes were crunched, reams and reams of data analysed in
a flash. A life was balanced, weighed, judged and a passport was
issued for The Politician – a passport straight to Hell:

Dear The Politician,

Congratulations on your recent death and thank you for your
interest in joining God and his Angelic Cohort in Heaven.
Regretfully, I have to inform that on this occasion your application

has not been successful. However, alternative accommodation has been found for you in Hell.

> *We very much hope you enjoy your stay.*
> *Yours eternally,*
> *The Heavenly Bureaucracy.*

So far, so good, you think, an evil individual dispatched to Hell. That's as it should be, is it not?

Not quite.

For you see, upon reaching Hell, The Politician, rather than being terrified and suffering, found it all rather convivial. Everywhere The Politician looked pain and suffering could be found. People being boiled alive, people being forced to watch as their intestines were ripped out, people rolling boulders up never-ending hills whilst being ferociously whipped, people being savagely raped by horse-hung and hugely tumescent demons and, worst of all, people chained to the spot and forced to listen to 'One Direction' songs played on a continuous (continuous as in *for all eternity)* loop...

As both a Connoisseur And Expert in pain and suffering and someone who had developed and enjoyed extreme appetites in all senses of the expression, The Politician found this fascinating, exciting and really quite wonderful – forgetting the humiliation of a political career ending in abject failure, imprisonment, sentencing and the terror and pain of hanging and the irreconcilable strangeness of death (which, it seemed, wasn't really death), The Politician decided that dying hadn't actually been that bad and that being sent to hell was, basically, Hitting The Jackpot!

And The Politician followed The Politician's nature and got to thinking. Here was a chance to take the habits of a lifetime into death and beyond, for The Politician's nature was that of all of that kind, the kind that set themselves to rule over others. The Politician was a psychopath, a creature that always, always wanted more. A creature of vile and despicable desires. A creature that would always put itself first at the expense of others, a creature obsessed with power and its own greed – one that lived and functioned solely to satisfy these needs, oblivious to the consequences for ordinary people who are, after all, but a detail in history. Sheep to the slaughter. Chickens for plucking.

How best then to slaughter these particular sheep, pluck these particular chickens?

What happens next? Buy the book and find out!

Milton Keynes UK
Ingram Content Group UK Ltd.
UKHW010719140823
426838UK00001B/16